8/98-16- 8/98

LOS GATOS PUBLIC LIBRARY
Telephone: 408-354-6891

A fine shall be charged each day an item is kept overtime. No item will be issued to persons in arrears for fines.

Loss of, or damage to an item other than regular wear and tear, must be paid by the person to whom the book is charged.

Attention is called to the rule that items borrowed from the library must not be loaned.

For violation of these rules, the privileges of the library may be withdrawn from any person at any time.

GAYLORD F

For Grandpa,
Edward Arthur Reilly,
with love

Rosie's Nutcracker Dreams

BALLET SLIPPERS™ 2

Rosie's Nutcracker Dreams
by Patricia Reilly Giff

illustrated by Julie Durrell

VIKING

Thank you to Doris Driver, Director of the New England
Academy of Dance in New Canaan, Connecticut

VIKING
Published by the Penguin Group
Penguin Books USA Inc., 375 Hudson Street, New York, New York 10014, U.S.A.
Penguin Books Ltd, 27 Wrights Lane, London W8 5TZ, England
Penguin Books Australia Ltd, Ringwood, Victoria, Australia
Penguin Books Canada Ltd, 10 Alcorn Avenue, Toronto, Ontario, Canada M4V 3B2
Penguin Books (N.Z.) Ltd, 182-190 Wairau Road, Auckland 10, New Zealand

Penguin Books Ltd, Registered Offices: Harmondsworth, Middlesex, England

First published in 1996 by Viking, a division of Penguin Books USA Inc.

1 3 5 7 9 10 8 6 4 2

Text copyright © Patricia Reilly Giff, 1996
Illustrations copyright © Penguin Books USA Inc., 1996
All rights reserved

LIBRARY OF CONGRESS CATALOGING-IN-PUBLICATION DATA
Giff, Patricia Reilly.
Rosie's Nutcracker dreams / by Patricia Reilly Giff ; illustrated by Julie Durrell.
p. cm. — (Ballet slippers ; 2)
Summary : A clash with her rival may end Rosie's dream of playing
the leading role in her ballet class's production of the Nutcracker.
ISBN 0-670-86865-5 (hardcover)
[1. Ballet—Fiction. 2. Conduct of life—Fiction. 3. Family life—Fiction.]
I. Durrell, Julie, ill. II. Title. III. Series : Giff, Patricia Reilly. Ballet slippers ; 2.
PZ7.G3626Ros 1996 [Fic]—dc20 96-15254 CIP AC

Printed in U.S.A.
Set in OptiBrite

Chapter 1

It was almost dark. I could see a pale moon, and a few snowflakes falling.

We were building a fort at the curb—Murphy and me. It was a perfect hiding place if anyone came around the corner.

"If only we had a hose, Rosie." Murphy peeled off his mittens. They were thick with snow. "We could ice up the whole fort. It would be here for the rest of the winter."

I didn't say anything. I wasn't talking, and Murphy knew it.

"Rosie . . ." he began again, frowning. His face was red from the cold, and his big ears were sticking out of his green hat.

I started to laugh. I pointed to his face, his ears, his freezing hands.

"Stop that," he said, "and start talking."

I shook my head *no.* I began to roll up a snowball in case Robert Ray came around the corner.

It was only about five o'clock. And I wasn't going to say one word until the bank chimes went off at six.

"Mime." I made the word with my lips, without making a sound.

"This ballet stuff is getting to be a pain," Murphy said.

I pressed my lips together. I could feel how chapped they were. Murphy knew as well as I did that ballet was the most important thing in my life.

This afternoon, Miss Deirdre had told us we

6

were going to do *The Nutcracker* this winter. The whole thing would be dancing and miming, telling the story of Clara. I couldn't wait.

I looked up at Amy Stetson's window. Amy was older, thirteen, and almost a real ballerina. I could see her practicing. She was doing a *plié*.

"Toes out," she'd say. "Straight down, bending your knees out. And then up, straight up."

I had tried it a hundred times. "You have to think of a toaster," she told me. "You're the piece of bread popping straight up. If one thing sticks out... chin ... bottom ..." She shuddered. "You're burnt toast."

Right now a car was coming up the street. I grabbed Murphy's sleeve, and pulled him behind the fort. I opened my mouth as if I were screaming. I raised my hands high over my head.

Murphy still didn't get it.

"Robbers coming," I said. "Can't you tell anything?" Then I snapped my mouth shut, and bit my chapped lips.

Murphy was laughing. "You talked," he said.

His father pulled their car into the driveway. The Murphys would be having supper in about two minutes.

We'd be eating soon, too. The lights were on in our kitchen, and I could see the top of Grandpa's head at the table. His crossword puzzle would be in front of him.

I felt a little worm of worry. Something was wrong with Grandpa lately, but I didn't know what. When I asked my mother, she had just brushed my bangs back. "Don't worry, Rosaleen," she said.

I leaned against the fort again, dreaming about being a ballet star. Grandpa had taken me to see *The Nutcracker* last year. Our seats were in the back, and when I had seen Clara, the star, I got up and danced in the aisle.

I thought about wearing a white net tutu with diamonds. I thought about being Clara, and about the Nutcracker my uncle had just given me. It was a wooden army officer with a painted red coat. Its jaw opened wide and closed to crack the nuts.

"Rosie..." Murphy poked his face up to my nose. "Someone's coming around the corner."

Robert Ray, I bet. He was probably wheeling a wagonful of snowballs, ready for war.

We were ready, too.

But before I saw it was the wrong kind of body for Robert, taller and rounder, I had let go of my first snowball.

It had been sitting around for so long, it was almost an iceball.

Murphy let go of two of his.

"Yeowwww!" someone screeched, and disappeared around the corner again.

"Bull's-eye!" I yelled, forgetting about mime.

"Yes!" Murphy shouted. He peered over the fort. "Who was that anyway?"

I raised my shoulders in the air, and rolled

my eyes. A perfect mime answer: *I don't know.*

I could hear the kid, still yelling, halfway up Orient Street.

Mrs. Murphy poked her head out their door. "Dinner, Tommy."

Murphy made gagging sounds. He fell back on top of the fort. "Mime." He grinned at me. "It means we're having veal things for supper."

I watched him trudge up his driveway. The streetlights had just come on. Then I stood on top of the fort, and started a *plié.* I tried to make it as good as Amy's.

First I turned my toes out, and went down straight, bending my knees, thighs out . . .

Then, up, straight up.

Across the street, Amy's window opened. "You're burnt toast," she called, laughing.

I looked up.

"Don't worry," she said. "You'll get there."

I knew it. I had to get there.

I was going to practice like crazy. If I got the

part of Clara in *The Nutcracker*, I'd never ask for anything again.

My little brother, Andrew, knocked on the window. "Supper, Rosie," I could almost hear him say.

I did one more *plié*, then headed up our driveway for supper. I went in the back door, wondering who we had blasted with the snowballs.

Chapter 2

If I didn't rush around like crazy, I'd be late for tryouts. And it was all because of Murphy.

Murphy had found a hose. Well, not really a hose. He had found a watering can in his garage.

We had spent an hour filling it with water in Murphy's kitchen, and lugging it out to the fort. Back and forth a hundred times.

Murphy was right. The fort was solid ice now.

So were our hands.

In my bedroom, I grabbed my pink tights and scoop-neck leotard with long sleeves. The tights were ripped; the leotard had chocolate stains. I shoved them into the blue bag marked ROSIE O'MEARA, BALLET. KEEP OUT, THIEVES.

And then, carefully, on top, I put in my pink ballet slippers from Grandpa.

They were the best, absolutely.

I stopped to catch my breath, and to take a quick look in the mirror. No one would know I was afraid. My face looked like its regular self. My heart was beating fast, though. I could see the little *bump-bump* of it on the side of my neck.

I turned to see what I could of the back of my head. I was trying to grow a ballerina bun. Amy said that a real ballerina had to have a bun. "A must," she said. "You know, for a swan's neck."

I didn't know, but I didn't want to ask a million questions every two minutes.

Too bad Albert the barber had chopped my hair off again last month. The ends were only half an inch long. I knew because Murphy had pulled a bunch out to measure them for me.

I looked up at the picture over my bed. It was a black-and-white photograph of my beautiful grandmother, Genevieve. She was doing a *grand battement.* She wore feathers and a white tutu. I talked to her all the time.

Outside, I could hear yelling—even with the windows closed. It was Karen Cooper. "Rooooosssssiiiieeee!" she yelled.

Karen had the loudest mouth in Lynfield.

"Good grief," I heard Grandpa saying in the kitchen. "That kid looks so tiny, but she could wake the dead."

I rubbed at the frost on the window. Karen was standing on the front path, and across the street, Stephanie Witt was racing by.

Stephanie was a little weird. So were her

four older brothers and two older sisters. All she ever did was draw pictures... on paper, with chalk on the sidewalk, and on the side of her garage.

She took a quick look at Karen and then at my window. She probably wanted to be sure she was going to beat us to ballet practice. "I'm coming!" I yelled to Karen through the closed window, and watched Stephanie pick up speed.

Quickly I covered my mouth. My little brother Andrew was supposed to be taking a nap.

"Good grief," Grandpa said in the kitchen.

I looked up at the picture again. I stood in just the right spot, at the end of the bed. I could catch Genevieve's eyes there. It seemed as if she looked down, smiling at me.

"I want to be Clara," I whispered. I raised my arms, miming Clara reaching for the Nutcracker.

16

"Who's Clara?" Andrew padded into my bedroom, wearing his fuzzy bear slippers.

"She's in a story," I told him. "Her uncle gives her a Nutcracker, and her little brother breaks it."

"Not me," Andrew said, following me into the kitchen.

Grandpa rolled his eyes. "Ah, Andrew," he said. "That was the fastest nap in history. Four and a half minutes."

"Sorry," I said. "My fault."

Grandpa smiled. He reached into his pocket and pulled a dollar out for me. "Stop for cocoa on the way back."

"Thanks." I said, trying to smile. This was probably the most important afternoon of my life. How could I think of cocoa?

"Bring me a cocoa, too, Rosie." Andrew pulled on my ballet bag. "Extra, extra whipped cream."

The most important afternoon, and inside

17

the bag, my tights had a rip and my leotard a stain.

Andrew pulled at me harder, yelled louder. "Say yes or no."

"I can't carry cocoa all the way home, Andrew," I said, frowning.

Andrew frowned right back. "That's another lie, Rosie."

"Don't worry," Grandpa told him. "We're going to get on our boots, and go for our own cocoa."

"See," Andrew told me.

I leaned over to give him a kiss. Then I was out the door, with Grandpa calling, "May the wind be at your back, Rosie," and Andrew asking, "What does that mean again?"

I waved, listening to Grandpa. "The wind will push her along, make her go faster, easier."

"But why?"

The wind was whistling around me. "For good luck," I could hear Grandpa saying.

Karen was stamping on a snow pile. She clicked her teeth as if she were riding a horse. "Finally," she said. "I'm turning into an ice cube."

We galloped toward Scranton Avenue, Karen and me—galloped because Karen was a horse person, even though she had never been on a horse in her life.

"Shortcut," I said. "Down the alley."

We went the back way behind the stores. In three steps, we knew it was a mistake. We sank into snow over our boots. "Yeow!" I yelled.

We kept going, though. We circled the pile of cartons in back of Hot Bagels, and clumped to a stop at Dance with Miss Deirdre.

Even though we had only two seconds to spare, I took a deep breath, and counted to seven. Slowly. That's what Grandpa always told me to do when I didn't know an answer on a test. "Clears your mind," he said. "Helps you think."

I had to have a clear mind. I had to think. It would be terrible if I didn't get a wonderful part. Terrible for me, because I loved to dance.

But more terrible for Grandpa.

I knew Grandpa was counting on it.

Chapter 3

Stephanie Witt had gotten there first.

Of course.

She was holding onto the barre as hard as she could. She wanted to be sure she had the best spot, right in the middle.

She made a face at me. A horrible face, showing a missing front tooth.

"What's the matter with you?" I said.

She didn't answer.

"Pumpkin face," I said, but under my breath. It might be bad luck to be mean. I watched her doing a *plié*. In a toaster, she'd be burned to a crisp.

Then I looked around. Other kids were at the barre, holding on lightly to practice the positions. Slivers of slush from everyone's boots were all over the wooden floor.

Miss Deirdre would have a fit.

I raced into the changing room with Karen and threw on my stuff. I put the leotard on backward so no one would see the chocolate stain, and held my hand over the rip in the tights.

Then I grabbed a place at the barre, halfway along the line, next to Karen. I held on with both hands so no one could push me down further.

I took a quick look to be sure Miss Deirdre wasn't there yet. She always said we had to be polite if we wanted to stay. Polite and kind.

Miss Serena was playing music on the piano. It was *Nutcracker* music. Every once in a while, she'd raise one hand from the keys and push her frizzy red hair out of her face. When she did, I could see bits of gray in her bangs.

Poor Miss Serena was a mess . . . until she smiled. Then her whole face changed.

Something at the back window caught my eye. It was green, but the window was so steamed over, it was hard to see.

I didn't have time to think about that. Miss Deirdre danced into the studio. Miss Deirdre was beautiful. Today she was wearing a red leotard with white leg warmers, a white ribbon around her bun, and red nail polish . . . really red, the kind I always wished my mother wore.

Miss Deirdre waved one hand. That meant we should sit on the floor, and listen *seer-ee-us-ly*.

I sank down in front of the barre and put on my most serious face.

Underneath me, the slush was turning to water . . . water that was soaking me right through to the skin. I tried not to pay attention. I tried not to move.

Besides *seer-ee-us-ness*, Miss Deirdre liked *stilll-nesss* when she was talking.

And she was getting to the important stuff. She needed kids to play the part of the Nutcracker, and toys, and mice, and, of course, Clara.

My grandmother Genevieve had danced in *The Nutcracker*, and Grandpa had promised to show me the pieces from the newspaper. I knew she must have been a beautiful dancer.

From the corner of my eye, I could see something at the window again. Someone was rubbing a hand across the pane, trying to see in.

I took a tiny hitch toward Karen to see.

Murphy. Spying.

When he saw me looking, he yanked his green wool hat down over his eyebrows. He knew he could make me laugh. He could always make me laugh.

"Right, Rosaleen?" Miss Deirdre said.

I took a breath, and guessed. "Yes."

Miss Deirdre smiled, and looked happy, so I knew I had said the right thing.

At the piano, I could see that Miss Serena didn't look happy. She looked sad. I leaned forward a little. It felt as if I were sliding around on ice water.

But there wasn't time to think about Miss Serena, or Murphy at the window.

Miss Deirdre raised one hand in the air. She waved her fingers as she spoke. "Who's first?" she asked.

Miss Serena played a couple of tinkling sounds on the piano.

Before I could lose my courage, I jumped up. I had practiced a hundred times, a thousand times. But this time was different. This time I really needed the wind at my back.

And in the mirror, I could see the whole back of me was wet.

And up above, Murphy was laughing.

I wasn't laughing. Besides stains and rips and a wet leotard, I had other things to worry about. One of them was trying to do a perfect *grand jeté* while I was miming sadness. I was Clara, and the Nutcracker was broken.

And the other thing to worry about was Stephanie Witt. She had plunked herself down at the barre. There she was, sitting right in front of me.

I narrowed my eyes at her, but she didn't pay attention. "Out of the way," I said. She just blinked.

Could I help it if I *grand jeté*d right into her lap?

Chapter 4

It was almost dark by the time ballet lessons were over. Too late for cocoa. Karen was afraid of kidnappers.

Murphy had gone halfway through the try-outs. They ate early in his house. He was supposed to be inside, at the table, at five o'clock sharp.

Karen and I galloped back along Scranton Avenue.

"Stop looking over your shoulder," I said.

"There are people all over the place, and not one criminal."

"You were really good today," Karen said, making me feel wonderful.

"You were good, too," I said back, crossing my fingers. Then I thought of my own *grand jeté*, and sailing into Stephanie's lap.

"Oof!" Stephanie had yelled like a big baby. She had limped off into the bathroom crying. "You ruined everything again, Rosie," she said, over her shoulder.

She was still crying ten minutes later, telling everyone she'd never get to be Clara because I had dented in her thighs.

How did she think she'd ever get to be Clara anyway? She fell over every time she had to raise one foot off the floor.

Karen wound her way around the telephone pole on Five Corners. "Yes," she told me, "I bet you get a good part."

"Like..." I said, crossing my fingers.

She stopped to think.

I wished she didn't have to think for so long. I couldn't stop shivering.

"What's that thing you get when you're freezing?" I asked.

"Mmm...frostbite?"

Exactly. I'd have to tell Grandpa.

Grandpa would be waiting for me. He would be doing the crossword puzzle at the kitchen table. My mother would be starting supper.

"Well, Rosie-o," he'd say. "How was the practice?"

I closed my eyes for a moment. I tried to think if I had been bad or good . . . after the *grand jeté* mess, I mean.

A girl named Joy had been the best, I thought, feeling worried.

Stephanie had been the worst.

I sighed. I was probably somewhere in between.

"About that part," I said, trying to remind Karen. "What do you think I'll get?"

I didn't look at her. If only she said *Clara*.

We started to walk again. We had about ten steps to Karen's corner. Before she could say a word, we heard someone calling.

Halfway down the block, Karen's mother was standing on their front steps. "Hurry up," she called. "Nana's on the phone from Brooklyn. She wants to say hello."

Karen gave me a little wave. She took off over the snow piles on Nancy Place.

Then she looked back. "Clara!" she called. "I know you'll be Clara."

I stood there, watching her slip across the snow. Murphy had been my best friend since I was three years old. And Karen had lived in Lynfield for only a few months. I was lucky to have two friends. I felt a warm feeling in my chest, the syrup of happiness my teacher, Mrs. Hamilton, talked about sometimes.

Then I walked the rest of the way home.

I loved to walk when it was almost dark. Everyone's living-room lights were coming on. Kids were running back and forth in their playrooms. Televisions were flickering.

Mrs. Brockfast was shoveling her walk on the next block. You could hear the clink of the shovel when it hit the sidewalk under the snow.

And no one was very close to me. I could talk to myself aloud. "Maybe I really was the best," I said. I slid down the snow in front of Murphy's house.

I could see the light in our living-room window. Andrew was standing on top of the couch, ready to jump off. His lips were moving, and he was counting: *"eight, nine, ten, forty-eleven…"*

Watching him, I could feel the syrup of happiness disappearing. Something was bothering me. Not about Andrew. About Stephanie.

"You'll be sorry," Stephanie had told me, still crying a little, at the end of tryouts.

But she had sounded like Andrew.

I hated it when Andrew cried. I hated to see his eyes filled with tears, his mouth drooping.

That's the way Stephanie had looked.

I stood there, feeling bad for another moment. Then I stamped my boots to get the snow off. I went slowly into the house.

Chapter 5

"And then what?" Andrew asked.

I twirled around, did a *plié*, straight as a pin, and a *grand jeté*, and slid five plates onto the table. Mom, Dad, Grandpa, Andrew, me. "Then what... what?" I asked him.

"What happened after Clara's brother broke the Nutcracker?" He followed me around the table with the salt and pepper shakers.

"Clara went to bed," I said. "She felt terrible ... so terrible she couldn't sleep. She sneaked downstairs again to see how bad it was."

"And it wasn't bad at all," said Andrew. "I knew it."

"It *was* bad," I said. "The Nutcracker's poor jaw was broken. And worse than that, suddenly an army of huge gray mice ran across the floor after him. Like this…"

I chased Andrew around the table, and grabbed him, tickling his neck.

Grandpa was smiling at me. I had told him all about the tryouts the minute I had come in.

He had danced around the kitchen, too, tall and a little stiff. "You were good," he said. "I'm not surprised. You're like Genevieve, your grandmother."

Right now he was singing, "It's a great day for the Irish…"

"Too loud, Grandpa," Andrew said.

"Sorry." Grandpa winked at me.

My mother started to sing. "Humm, humm, great day—" and stopped. "I wish I had more tomatoes."

"Come on, Rosie," Grandpa said. "We'll march ourselves down to my office in the basement. I have Genevieve's newspaper clippings somewhere."

I followed Grandpa down the stairs, watching him hit the light switch. We walked through to the back, to the tiny room he called his office.

It was filled with tools. Pictures of Genevieve were pinned up on the wall over his workbench. And underneath were a million boxes.

"Don't worry," Grandpa told me. "Next summer I'm going to put labels on every box. In the meantime, we'll just have to look through..."

Upstairs, I could hear the door. My father was home.

"Dinner will be in three minutes," I said, trying to make him find everything in a hurry.

Grandpa never hurried. While he rooted

around underneath, I looked up at Genevieve's pictures ... and looked closer.

In one of them she was up on her toes, her head bent, her hair up in a bun ... and for the first time I saw what Amy meant about a swan's neck. Genevieve's neck was long and delicate like a swan's.

I felt my own neck. It was long, too. If only my hair was long enough to twist up, maybe I'd look like a ballerina.

Grandpa pulled out the first box. It was filled with old pieces of paper and envelopes. All of them blank.

Grandpa nodded at me. "Just in case I ever write a letter." He shook his head. "I don't have anyone to write to."

I thought he sounded sad. I looked up. His face looked the way it always did, smiling lines around his blue eyes, his nose beautiful and straight.

Next came a box of shirts. "Ssh," Grandpa

said. "Christmas presents from everyone for the last four years. I have a million shirts."

Over my head, I could hear footsteps. Andrew's, quick and light. My mother's, heels clicking. And my father's, heavy, still in his boots.

I could hear the phone ringing.

Grandpa looked up. "I don't know what's the matter with people, calling at supper time."

He fished through another box. "Old magazines," he said. "I wondered where they were."

I was dying for him to find the right box before supper.

Too late, I thought. I heard Andrew come to the top of the stairs.

"Mommy wants you," Andrew called. "You, Rosie. You're in lots of trouble."

I laughed. "That's another lie, Andrew."

It wasn't a lie.

We went up the stairs. Grandpa and me. My mother had stopped making dinner.

41

She was standing at the table, waiting.

My father was waiting, too.

"What happened at ballet lessons?" my mother asked.

"Tryouts," I said. "Don't you remember?"

"That was Miss Deirdre," my mother said. "Someone's mother called and said you—"

Stephanie Witt, I thought in an instant. I remembered the *grand jeté* into her lap.

I began to shake my head. "No. It was an accident."

My mother went back to the stove. "And what about the ice ball?"

"What ice ball?" I said. "I never—"

"Rosie doesn't tell lies," Andrew said.

Suddenly I remembered the other after-noon, someone coming around the corner…

My mother began to spoon peas into a bowl.

I closed my eyes. Bull's-eye.

My mother missed with a spoonful of peas.

A couple of them skittered onto the floor. "Stephanie . . ." my mother began. "Is that her name?"

I nodded. My mouth felt dry. Everyone was looking at me. My father was shaking his head, and my mother had two spots of red on her neck.

Grandpa didn't look upset, though. He looked angry. "Rosie wouldn't—"

"No," Andrew said. "Never."

"Stephanie was on her way to a birthday party." My mother put the bowl of peas on the table. "Her hair was soaking wet, and she had a mark on her cheek all week."

I had a picture of Stephanie in my mind. Stephanie going to a birthday party. One tooth was missing, and her hair was all in twisty curls.

I began to feel sorry for her again. But my mother was saying something else. Something terrible.

"Miss Deirdre thinks you shouldn't come to lessons for a while." My mother looked sad, as if she were going to cry. "Miss Deirdre says she wants her students to be—"

I finished it for her. "Polite," I said softly. "And kind."

Grandpa slid into his place at the table. "Ridiculous. I'll go over there tomorrow and—"

"Stephanie wanted to be Clara," my mother was saying.

I swallowed. Stephanie wasn't good enough to be Clara. Joy maybe, or Maureen, or Kelly. I sighed. I wasn't going to be Clara, either.

My mother put the rest of the dinner on the table. Mashed potatoes. Cut-up tomatoes. Chicken with lovely dark skin.

My favorites. And I remembered something Grandpa had told me once about Genevieve.

When she was eight, she had gotten in trouble. Grandpa hadn't remembered why. Her mother had given her lamb chops for supper that night, a dinner that she had always loved.

But even when she was grown, even when she was Genevieve with a swan's neck, she never ate lamb again.

I looked at the chicken with the crispy skin, and the peas, and tomatoes.

I didn't think I'd eat any of that ever again.

Chapter 6

Last night, I heard Andrew crying, screaming. I wasn't the only one. Everyone else rushed to his bedroom.

"It's only a dream," we all told him. "A nightmare."

Andrew held out his arms to me . . . not to anyone else. He wrapped them around my neck. I could feel his whole body shaking.

"It was the mice," he told me. "They were after me."

"Oh, Andrew." I patted his back. "You're

thinking about *The Nutcracker.*"

He held me tighter, gulping. He tried to catch his breath.

"Listen," I told him. "When the mice army attacked, all the toy soldiers helped the Nutcracker win. They *grand jeté*d after those mice with their swords..."

"Really?" His eyes were closing.

"Really. And then the Nutcracker took Clara across the Lemonade Ocean to the Land of the Sweets."

"Mmm." Andrew was already asleep as I helped him lie back against the pillows.

My mother nodded at me. "You're a very nice girl, Rosie," she said in an Andrew voice.

And my father smiled. "Let's all go back to bed," he said.

It seemed as if morning came only two minutes later. I went down to breakfast yawning.

I felt terrible. I kept thinking about Clara. I'd

never get to travel across the Lemonade Ocean to the Land of the Sweets.

Everyone else looked sad, too. My father gave me an extra piece of toast with strawberry jam.

Andrew told me to be a trainman instead of a ballerina.

Grandpa patted my hand. "Don't worry," he said. "I'm going over after breakfast. I'll talk to Miss Deirdre. You'll see. Everything will turn out all right."

"Poor, poor Rosie," Andrew said, his mouth filled with toast.

But my mother shook her head. "Let's not forget something here."

We all looked up.

"Rosie was wrong."

Grandpa blew his breath out between his teeth. "Well…"

"I didn't mean…" I began.

"No," said Andrew.

I swallowed. No one said a word. Outside I could hear a truck sanding Mildred Place.

Then my father nodded. "Mom is right."

I sat there looking down at my toast.

In a voice so soft I could hardly hear her, my mother was saying something else. "You'll have to tell Stephanie you're sorry."

I began to shake my head *no* before my mother finished.

"I hate Stephanie Witt," I said. "And besides, she said I'd be sorry."

"But Rosie," my mother said, her hand on my shoulder. "People's feelings are important. You really hurt Stephanie."

I stuck out my lip the way Andrew did sometimes.

But then so did my mother. "Yes," she said. "Even if Grandpa talks Miss Deirdre into letting you come back," she said. "Otherwise..."

I took a look at my mother's face. I knew she wouldn't change her mind.

A quick flash of Genevieve came into my head. Genevieve dancing around the Nutcracker. Genevieve as Clara.

I would never be Clara.

I would never be anybody.

And something else. I wouldn't tell Stephanie I was sorry, in a hundred years. Not in a million years.

Chapter 7

Outside it was warm, and so sunny it seemed that diamonds were twinkling on the piles of snow. We were packing snow on top of the fort, Murphy and me.

I put my face up to the sun. I made believe none of this had happened with ballet. I stood like a swan, my neck long and delicate, with one arm stretched out, and fingers pointed the way Amy did.

"Pretend your fingers are curved just a little,"

she'd say. "Pretend they're being held up gently on strings."

Across the street, our front door opened. It was Grandpa. He was dressed in his best clothes. A long blue coat. A gray hat with a tiny feather.

"Whooeee," said Murphy. "Sunday clothes."

"Grandpa's going to ask Miss Deirdre to let me come back," I told him.

"Think it will work?" Murphy asked.

I sighed. "Miss Deirdre is pretty strict. Besides..." I stopped. I had told Murphy everything except having to say I was sorry.

"This whole ballet thing is getting to be a pain in the neck," Murphy said.

We watched Grandpa going up the street, very tall and a little bent. He didn't see us behind the fort. He didn't even look.

"May the wind be at your back, Grandpa," I whispered.

"What...?" Murphy began.

I waved my hand. "For luck."

Murphy wasn't paying attention. He was adding slushy snow to the top of the fort.

A moment later, his father came out. He and Murphy were going to the father-son day at the firehouse.

"Finish this up?" Murphy slapped a last lump of slush on the fort. "Yes or no?"

"Yes." I nodded.

I worked on the fort alone, until I saw Grandpa come up the block.

By that time, the sun had gone. I didn't want to go into the house, though. Grandpa had walked up the path slowly. His head was bent, and a plaid scarf covered his chin. I couldn't see his face.

I picked up a clean scoop of snow and tasted it, thinking about Grandpa. Lately, Grandpa looked sad. He wasn't singing "Rosie O'Grady" at me every morning. He hadn't finished his crossword puzzle in days.

Across the street, Andrew was banging on the kitchen window. He yelled something, but I didn't know what.

Then I realized. "*I'm telling*," he was saying.

I grinned at him, and dropped the snow. Andrew was the worst tattletale in the world. I could almost see him running to tell Grandpa. "*Rosie's eating snow again. Dirty snow. Germy snow. She's going to get sick and die.*"

I almost wished I was sick with something like that thing Murphy had told me about where your arms and legs fall off. I tried to think of who'd cry if that happened to me. Would Miss Deirdre, or pumpkin-face Stephanie with her wiry curls?

I thought about going to Karen's, but I'd have to tell her I was out of ballet. So I just walked along the snow piles to the end of Mildred Place and turned the corner onto Orient Street.

A mess of kids were on the next corner. The

Witt kids. They were sliding up and down on the ice in their driveway, yelling and screaming.

I went by on the other side of the street with my nose in the air. I didn't want to take one look at the Witts. Especially not at pumpkin-face Stephanie who had ruined my life.

I said it under my breath, hardly moving my lips. "Stephanie Witt has ruined my life."

I snorted. And my mother wanted me to say I was sorry.

Just before I turned the corner, I looked back. Stephanie wasn't sliding around with the rest of the Witts. She was sitting on her steps, looking at me.

I just kept going. By this time, I was freezing cold. My feet were blocks of ice. I started back up Orient Street. Stephanie was probably thinking about her chance to be Clara in *The Nutcracker.*

Some Clara.

She didn't look all excited, I thought. She looked as if she were all alone. But that couldn't be. She had so many brothers and sisters.

I had to go home. I was absolutely going to freeze to death any minute.

I still didn't go home. I turned around and went down to the corner, and hid behind the telephone pole and a pile of snow.

Stephanie Witt was going to freeze to death, too. She hadn't moved a muscle since I had first seen her.

Chapter 8

I could hear Grandpa singing as soon as I opened the back door. "Her eyes are blue and her hair is curled…"

I took a deep breath. Grandpa sounded happy. Miss Deirdre must have…

Andrew marched across the kitchen in front of me. And he certainly wasn't singing. He was wearing his hat, his boots, and his underwear.

"You'll catch cold," I told him.

"I don't care." His lower lip stuck out a mile.

My mother rolled her eyes at me.

"What's the matter?" I asked.

Andrew didn't answer.

"Come on," I said.

He looked up at me. "I want to go out."

"It's snowing," I said. "It's cold."

"No one will take me," he said.

I thought about taking him, but my hands were probably frostbitten.

"Besides." He held up his fingers. "One. I don't have a fort. Two. I don't have a Murphy. Seven. I don't have anybody for a friend."

"Oh, Andrew . . ." I could feel my eyes getting blurry. This Saturday had to be the worst day of my whole life. "I'm your friend."

"A sister doesn't count," he said, and clumped away.

"What about Daddy? What about Grandpa?" I called after him.

He turned around. "That's a daddy. That's a grandpa. I said a *friend*."

I went down the cellar stairs. Grandpa was

moving boxes around. "I'm full of energy, Rosaleen Stringbean," he said. "I'm feeling the syrup of happiness."

"Did you see Miss Deirdre then?" I couldn't wait, now, to hear what had happened.

"I saw the beautiful one," he said.

"Miss Deirdre," I said.

Grandpa grinned at me. "I can't believe it. She never told me her name. We talked so long, and … Miss Deirdre … hmm."

I watched him rooting through his box of Christmas shirts. He held one up. It was a tan one with rusty little things like horses running all over it. Horrible.

"Nice," he said. "Very nice. I might just put it on and go down to the Kilkenny for dinner with Miss What's-her-name one of these days."

"But what happened?" I asked. "What about ballet lessons, and *The Nutcracker*?"

Grandpa blinked. "I'm sorry. Here you are waiting, and I'm going on about shirts…"

He looked serious for a moment. "She said she had to talk to the other one. Miss…"

"Serena," I said. "Whew. Miss Serena is wonderful."

I thought about Miss Serena. Did she think I had been mean to Stephanie on purpose? Even Miss Serena might not let me in.

I was so upset, it was hard to figure it out.

Andrew was coming down the stairs. "Did Clara really go to the Land of the Sweets?" he asked.

"Right to the Sugar Plum Fairy," I said. "Candy Canes danced, and Mrs. Bonbon danced with her children. Even the flowers waltzed in the garden."

"Wait a minute." Andrew was frowning. "She was dreaming. I bet there wasn't any Lemonade Ocean, or Candy Canes dancing."

"Well…" I said. "Clara wasn't sure, either." I took a breath. "Andrew, I'll tell you the rest later. I have to ask Grandpa something."

Grandpa was moving boxes around.

"What's going to happen next?" I asked.

Grandpa sat back on his h . "I just thought of something," he said. "If you don't tell Stephanie you're sorry, it won't make any difference."

I gulped.

Grandpa held up his hand. "Now I'm not saying you should say you're sorry. That has to come from the heart."

We didn't say anything for a minute.

"I have no one to play with," Andrew said, hopping off one of the boxes.

I looked at Grandpa.

"From the heart," he said. Then he ruffled Andrew's hair. "Who's that boy who lives on Scranton Avenue?"

Andrew put his hands over his eyes. "I'm thinking. Kyle?"

"We'll go over to Kyle's," Grandpa said. "We'll see if he wants to go with us for cocoa."

Grandpa ruffled my head, too. Then he went upstairs with Andrew.

I stood there thinking about Stephanie. How could I say I was sorry from my heart when I wasn't?

I pushed a couple of Grandpa's boxes out of the way, and went upstairs to the window, to watch Amy doing *grand jetés* across her bedroom floor.

Chapter 9

It must have been my turn to have a nightmare. It was mixed up with Clara, and a row of candy canes, and Andrew saying, "I don't have a Murphy. I don't have a friend."

I woke up crying. I could hear the wind rattling the windows. I pushed off the covers and slid out of bed, shivering.

It wasn't that late. I could hear Grandpa singing, "Her eyes are blue, la la, her hair is curled..."

Grandpa was happy again. I wondered why.

I went over to the window and looked out. It was almost as beautiful as the Land of the Sweets.

Thin icicles hung from the edge of Murphy's roof and all the tree branches. Our fort sparkled under the streetlight.

Then I was really crying again, and I didn't exactly know why. I could hear Grandpa beginning another song. "Casey would waltz with the strawberry blonde . . . " he sang in a deep voice.

I kept thinking about the nightmare. Suddenly, Stephanie Witt popped into my head. Stephanie painting ballerinas on the side of her garage last summer. I couldn't even remember if she had been in the dream.

I went out to the hall, past Andrew's bedroom. Andrew was a lump under his quilt, and Jake, our cat, was a ball on the end of the bed.

My mother and father's room came next.

When I was little like Andrew, I would have dived in with them and felt safe.

I took a deep breath, and counted to seven. *Clears your mind, helps you think,* I could almost hear Grandpa say.

I stood next to his door for a minute. He was wandering around inside, humming.

Then I went back to my own room and jumped into bed. I wiggled my feet around trying to find a warm spot, took a breath, and began to count again. One. Two...

And figured out why Grandpa was happy.

Andrew wasn't the only one who needed a friend. I thought about Miss Deirdre. Grandpa liked her. Why not? She was beautiful. I frowned a little. Not as nice as Miss Serena, I thought.

I twisted around to look up at Genevieve doing her *grand battement.* "Please don't mind," I whispered.

I couldn't imagine Grandpa taking Miss

Deirdre to Kilkenny's for dinner. He'd be wearing that terrible shirt with the rusty horses…

I started to count again. Three. Four. Five…

Stephanie didn't have any friends.

How did I think of that?

I could see her standing at the middle of the barre, all by herself. And what about the school yard? I'd never seen her with one person.

She didn't have a Murphy. She didn't have a fort. She didn't have a friend.

I fell asleep with the streetlight making shadows on the wall. I was thinking there was something I had to do in the morning. Something I had to ask Murphy.

I was the first one up. I didn't spend one extra minute in bed. I was absolutely glad it was Sunday and there wasn't any school.

Murphy was out ahead of me. He was on his way to the Crow's Nest Country Store to get the newspaper for his mother.

"Wait up," I called. "I have to ask you something. A favor."

"I don't have a cent," he said. "We can't get candy. We can't even get a gum ball."

I took a breath. "Could we share our fort?" I asked. "Just say yes or no."

"With Robert Ray, that nerd? No good."

I shook my head. "Not Robert. He has plenty of friends of his own."

The Crow's Nest Store was right in front of us. Murphy reached for the door. "You always do stuff like this, Rosie," he said. "Just when everything is going fine…"

I *grand jeté*d around him. "I knew you'd say yes," I said. "Thanks."

Murphy turned. "Andrew," he said. "I bet it's Andrew."

I just smiled. Then I headed home for breakfast. Grandpa would be frying potatoes with crispy edges, and thick slices of bacon.

"Not a very healthy breakfast," my mother said every Sunday.

And Grandpa always answered, "It's only one day a week, after all."

It was my favorite breakfast, and my mother's, too.

And I wasn't going to think about Stephanie Witt, or ballet, until I had finished every bite.

Chapter 10

After breakfast, I yanked on my boots, and *grand jeté*d out the door. "May the wind be at your back, Rosaleen O'Meara," I told myself.

I clumped down Mildred Place, and turned the corner onto Orient.

Two Witt kids were outside. I didn't know which two. A boy Witt, and a girl Witt, both a lot older than Stephanie.

I cleared my throat. "Is Stephanie here?"

"Pumpkin!" the girl screeched. She was even louder than Karen.

The boy looked at me and grinned. "She's missing a tooth. Knocked it out dancing. Danced right into the stair post."

"Poor—" I began.

"Terrible dancer. And now she has to go to the dentist."

"Hates the dentist," said the other Witt.

And then Stephanie was out the door. I couldn't see many wiry curls today. A red hat was smushed over her head. And she had thrown her jacket over her pajamas . . . pajamas with rusty-looking horses almost like Grandpa's.

I looked around. I didn't want those other Witts listening to what I had to say.

Especially since I didn't know exactly what I was going to say, anyway.

But I didn't have a chance to begin. "I'm sorry," Stephanie said. "I was going to tell you the other day, but I just couldn't get..."

I took a breath and counted to seven. It was

the fastest counting I had ever done in my life.

"I'm sorry from my heart," I told her. I didn't have to say I was sorry about *grand jeté*ing into her lap. That really was an accident.

Even the snowball had been meant for Robert Ray. And he wouldn't have minded one bit. He'd have tossed one back at me.

I especially didn't have to tell her what I was most sorry about. I was sorry that she didn't have a Murphy, or a fort, or a friend.

And I was going to try to fix all that.

But she was fixing something for me, too. "I know you should be Clara," she said. "You're great at mime. Great at ballet."

She pushed her hat back off her forehead. "I saw Miss Deirdre write your name down as Clara. I wanted to—" She broke off. "Maybe some other time."

I swallowed. "I'm out of ballet now."

Stephanie shook her head. "I'm sorry my mother called Miss Deirdre. And that's what I should have told you yesterday. I told Miss Deirdre it wasn't your fault, that I'd been hogging the barre."

"Really?" I kept nodding. I felt the sun warm on my face, and the syrup of happiness spreading in my chest.

"Yesterday," she said again. "When your grandfather was talking with Miss Serena. They were smiling and..."

Miss Serena. Grandpa had talked to the wrong one. I thought of Grandpa calling her beautiful. Of course. They'd be perfect friends. I could see them going to dinner at Kilkenny's, Grandpa wearing that shirt with the rusty horses.

"So anyway," Stephanie said. Her tongue came out of the little space where her tooth should be.

"So anyway," I said, too. And then I asked her. "Want to come over to our fort? Murphy's and mine?"

Stephanie was smiling. She looked as if she were feeling the syrup of happiness.

We'd play in the fort for a while. Then I was going inside. All afternoon I would dance in my living room. The rug would be the Lemonade Ocean, and the dining room the Land of the Sweets.

Then, maybe I would take Andrew for cocoa. I still had to tell him how Clara came down the next morning, and somehow the Nutcracker was shiny and new, and how she danced the ballet... feeling the syrup of happiness.

From Rosie's Notebook

Barre (say "BAR") It's a handrail in front of a mirror. Hold on and warm up!

Grand battement ("GRON baht-MA") A great kick. I haven't learned this yet, but Genevieve does it in the picture. One leg is thrown up in the air. It looks super!

Grand jeté ("GRON sheh-TAY") A leap! One leg is stretched forward, and one leg is back. This one looks great too.

Mime Use your face and hands and the rest of your body to tell a story.